Tooth Fairy Trouble
Hits Tinsel Tooth Town

written by SHANNON LYNN
illustrated by AARON POCOCK

Balboa Press books may be ordered through booksellers or by contacting:

Balboa Press
A Division of Hay House
1663 Liberty Drive
Bloomington, IN 47403
www.balboapress.com
1-(877) 407-4847

Because of the dynamic nature of the Internet, any web addresses or links contained in this book may have changed since publication and may no longer be valid. The views expressed in this work are solely those of the author and do not necessarily reflect the views of the publisher, and the publisher hereby disclaims any responsibility for them.

Certain stock imagery © Thinkstock.
Any people depicted in stock imagery provided by Thinkstock are models, and such images are being used for illustrative purposes only.

ISBN: 978-1-4525-3787-0 (sc)

Library of Congress Control Number: 2011915865

Printed in the United States of America

Balboa Press rev. date: 9/1/2011

To My Daughters, Shaniya and Shauntay,

and to ALL of the Wonderful Children

in this Great Big, Beautiful World.

For Miles and Miles, there were piles and piles of teeth. What would Tilly the tooth fairy do with all of those teeth? What could she do with all of those teeth? Tilly didn't know what to do, but she had to do something soon because if she didn't… the people of Tinsel Tooth Town would have to pack up and move!

Each night, Tilly traveled around the world and watched as the children hid their fallen teeth under their pillows, wishing for the tooth fairy to find them. When she flew down to gather those teeth, she tucked them into her special bag. Under each of their pillows, she placed a small token of love. She kissed her fingertips lightly and pressed them gently to their foreheads. "Sweet dreams my angels," she whispered, before flying off.

One evening, when it came time to return home, Tilly looked at the sack that hung heavily from her shoulder. A lump grew in her throat and the tears she'd been holding back flowed freely down her cheeks. Tilly struggled over to her favourite chair and then placed her head between her hands. "Whatever will I do with all of these teeth?" she sobbed.

As it awoke from a deep sleep, her tooth-filled bag began to wiggle and in a soft voice it spoke, "You can do anything, if only you'd try. Don't let your happiness just pass you by. Believe in yourself, do something! Be BOLD! And at the end of that rainbow… You just might find GOLD!" There was a moment of silence before it added, "So don't sit there and fret, now do as I say.

Get rid of those teeth… Where there's a will, there's a way!"

Tilly sprang to her feet. "Aha!" she shouted. "I have a plan!"
She raced to the kitchen, put some teeth in a pot and tried
popping them like popcorn. But, they wouldn't pop! And they
sure didn't taste like popcorn! YUCK! She spat out a tooth.

Tilly hurried into the living room and turned on the fireplace.
She toasted a tooth over that open fire and watched for it to puff
up soft and marshmallow mushy. But it wouldn't! And it didn't
taste like a marshmallow either! She spat out another tooth.

Tilly had been hoping to sell those special treats at the market; she was imagining carts and carts loaded with her tasty treasures! But, that wasn't going to happen.

Tilly paced back and forth. What could she do with all of those teeth?

"I'll make jewellery!" she cried. Tooth necklaces, bracelets and earrings!" Tilly pictured a factory filled with tons of teeth and spools of string strung everywhere. But, the more she thought about the tangled mess, the less she believed in it. "Maybe no one would wear teeth for jewellery," she said to herself. "And even if they did those with cavities would never sell."

Tilly scratched her forehead. "Aha! I have a much better idea! All of Tinsel Tooth Town will love this!"

The next morning, Tilly gathered the town's builders and explained her idea. They all huddled together before they scrambled off to spread the news.

That afternoon, all of Tinsel Tooth Town came
ready to help. And, even though it was a very
unusual idea, everyone cheered for its success!

The town's builders and the townspeople got busy. They sawed and they drilled. They glued and they shined. But after weeks of hard labour, it became clear that they had a new problem!

"Tilly," one of the builders shouted, "We're almost OUT of teeth!"

Tilly shook her head, not knowing what to do! All hope seemed lost.

Suddenly, a smile crept across her face. She had finally found the answer she had LONG searched for. "We did it!" she shouted to the crowd. "It's turned out even better this way! Tinsel Tooth Town will not ever be troubled again by too many teeth; the whole town can and will be a work in progress!"

Tilly and the townspeople danced around
with joy. When the last tooth was slipped
into place, the whole town cheered.

The results were stunning!

The piles and piles of teeth had become pieces to an enormous

TOOTH FAIRY CASTLE!

And from this day on, all of the streets and buildings in Tinsel Tooth Town are built from the many teeth that Tilly continues to collect.

Tilly worries about all of the sugar that children may eat, but she knows that the town dentists are there to help. And they will continue to keep those sugar bugs from creating harmful cavities that are filled with her secret recipe of tinsel and love.

CPSIA information can be obtained
at www.ICGtesting.com
Printed in the USA
246589LV00001B